This book belongs to...

....

....

The Nursery Collection

Animal Tales

This is a Parragon Book
This edition published in 2003

Parragon, Queen Street House, 4 Queen Street, Bath BA1 1HE, UK

Produced by The Templar Company plc

Cover designed by Shelley Doyle
Complied and edited by Caroline Repchuk
Designed by Kilnwood Graphics

Printed and bound in China
ISBN 1 40541 943 1

The Nursery Collection

Animal Tales

p

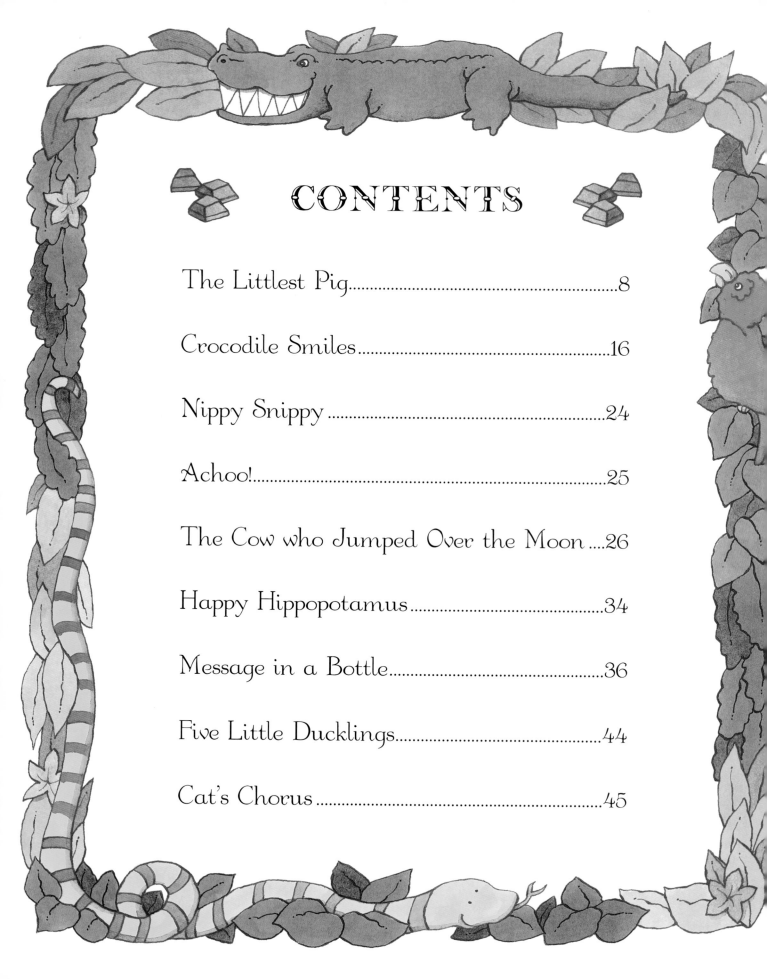

CONTENTS

The Littlest Pig..8

Crocodile Smiles...16

Nippy Snippy...24

Achoo!..25

The Cow who Jumped Over the Moon 26

Happy Hippopotamus...................................34

Message in a Bottle.......................................36

Five Little Ducklings......................................44

Cat's Chorus...45

Birthday Bunnies..46

High Jump..56

Lazy Lion..58

Elephants Never Forget...68

Itchy Spots..69

Whale Song...70

Little Sheep...78

Giraffe's Song...79

Leap Frog..80

Little Dog Lost..88

THE LITTLEST PIG

Little Pig had a secret. He snuggled down in the warm hay with his brothers and sisters, looked up at the dark sky twinkling with stars, and smiled a secret smile to himself. Maybe it wasn't so bad being the littlest pig after all...

Not so long ago, Little Pig had been feeling quite fed up. He was the youngest and by far the smallest pig in the family. He had five brothers and five sisters and they were all much bigger and fatter than he was. The farmer's wife called him Runt, as he was the smallest pig of the litter.

"I don't suppose little Runt will come to much," she told her friend Daisy, as they stopped by to bring the piglets some fresh hay.

His brothers and sisters teased him terribly.
"Poor little Runtie," they said to him, giggling.
"You must be the smallest pig in the world!"

"Leave me alone!" said Little Pig, and he crept
off to the corner of the pig pen, where he curled
into a ball, and started to cry. "If you weren't all
so greedy, and let me have some food, maybe I'd
be bigger!" he mumbled, sadly.

Every feeding time was the same – the others all pushed and shoved, and shunted Little Pig out of the way, until all that was left were the scraps. He would never grow bigger at this rate.

Then one day Little Pig made an important discovery. He was hiding in the corner of the pen, as usual, when he spied a little hole in the fence tucked away behind the feeding trough.

"I think I could fit through there!" thought Little Pig, excitedly.

He waited all day until it was time for bed, and then, when he was sure that all of his brothers and sisters were fast asleep, he wriggled through the hole. Suddenly he was outside, free to go wherever he pleased. And what an adventure he had!

First, he ran to the hen house and gobbled up the bowls of grain. Then he ran to the field, slipped under the fence, and crunched up Donkey's carrots.

He ran into the vegetable patch and munched a whole row of cabbages. What a wonderful feast! Then, when his little belly was full to bursting, he headed for home. On the way he stopped by the hedgerow. What was that lovely smell? He rooted around until he found where it was coming from – it was a bank of wild strawberries.

Little Pig had never tasted anything so delicious. "Tomorrow night, I'll start with these!" he promised himself as he trotted back home to the pig pen.

Quietly he wriggled back through the hole, and soon fell fast asleep snuggled up to his mother, smiling contentedly.

Night after night Little Pig continued his tasty adventures, creeping out through the hole when the others were sleeping. He no longer minded when they pushed him out of the way at feeding time, as he knew a much better feast awaited him outside. Sometimes he would find the farm dog's bowl filled with scraps from the farmer's supper, or buckets of oats ready for the horses. "Yum, yum — piggy porridge!" he would giggle, as he gobbled it up.

But as the days and weeks went by, and Little Pig grew bigger and fatter, it was more of a squeeze to wriggle through the hole each night.

Little Pig knew that soon he would no longer be able to fit through the hole, but by then he would be big enough to stand up to his brothers and sisters. And for now he was enjoying his secret!

CROCODILE SMILES

"Say cheese!" said the photographer.

"CHEESE!" grinned Snappy, the crocodile. Lights flashed, and cameras clicked as he gave his most winning smile.

"You're a natural!" cried the expedition leader. He was with a team of wildlife photographers. Snappy smiled at his reflection in the river.

"Ooh, you are a handsome chap!" he preened, gnashing his fine set of teeth together with glee.

Snappy was terribly proud of his sharp fangs, and fine good looks. He strutted up and down the riverbank for all to see.

"I'm a star!" he said. "My face will be known throughout the world!"

"Thanks for letting us take your picture," said the expedition leader.

"No problem," said Snappy. "Anytime!"

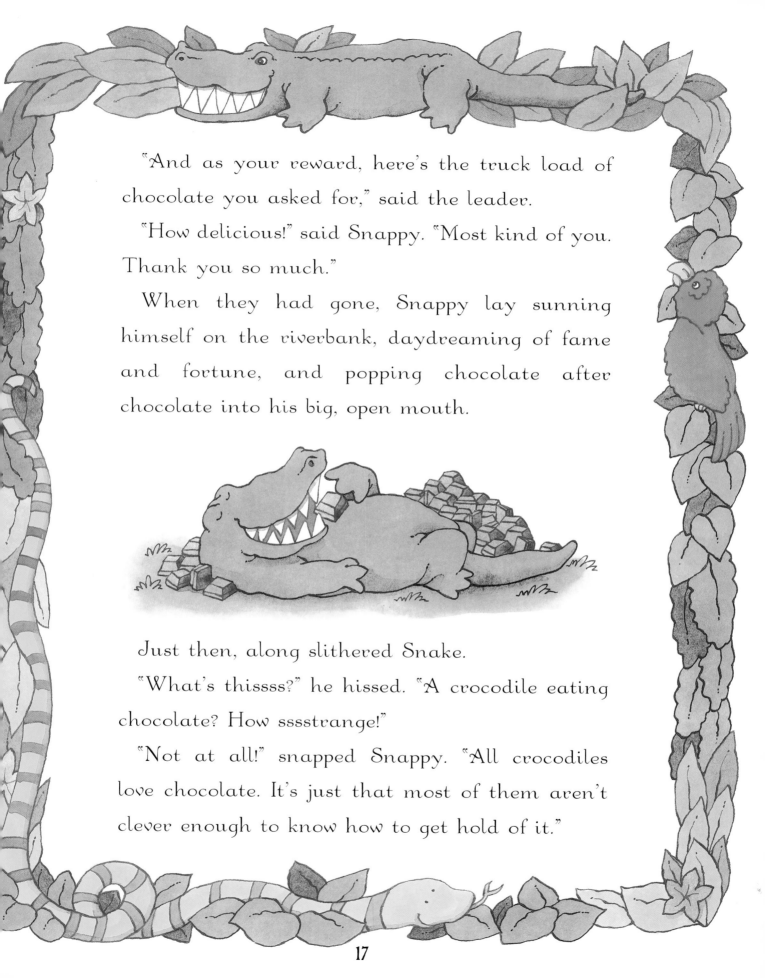

"And as your reward, here's the truck load of chocolate you asked for," said the leader.

"How delicious!" said Snappy. "Most kind of you. Thank you so much."

When they had gone, Snappy lay sunning himself on the riverbank, daydreaming of fame and fortune, and popping chocolate after chocolate into his big, open mouth.

Just then, along slithered Snake.

"What's thissss?" he hissed. "A crocodile eating chocolate? How sssstrange!"

"Not at all!" snapped Snappy. "All crocodiles love chocolate. It's just that most of them aren't clever enough to know how to get hold of it."

"Well, if you're so sssmart, you ssshould know that too much chocolate will make your teeth fall out!" hissed Snake.

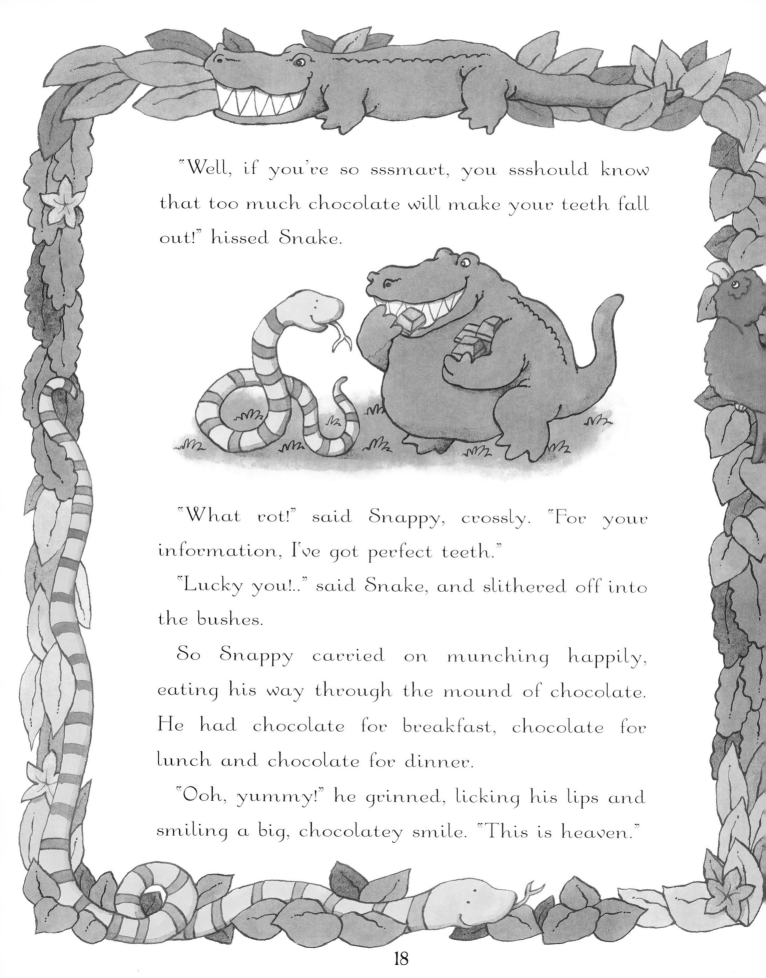

"What rot!" said Snappy, crossly. "For your information, I've got perfect teeth."

"Lucky you!.." said Snake, and slithered off into the bushes.

So Snappy carried on munching happily, eating his way through the mound of chocolate. He had chocolate for breakfast, chocolate for lunch and chocolate for dinner.

"Ooh, yummy!" he grinned, licking his lips and smiling a big, chocolatey smile. "This is heaven."

"You won't be saying that when you are too fat to float in the river," said parrot, who had been watching him from a tree.

"Nonsense!" scoffed Snappy. "I've got a very fine figure, I'll have you know!"

"If you say so," said Parrot, and flew off into the jungle.

Days and weeks passed, and Snappy happily carried on eating chocolate after chocolate, until at last it was all gone.

"Back to the river to catch my next meal, then," Snappy thought miserably. "Though I'd much rather have more chocolate!"

But when Snappy slid into the river, instead of bobbing gently at the surface, he sank straight to the bottom, and his stomach rested in the mud.

"Oh, dear, what's happened to the river?" Snappy wondered aloud to himself. "It's very hard to float in today."

"Even for someone with such a fine figure as you?" jeered Parrot, watching from the trees. Snappy didn't answer. He just sank further beneath the water so that only his two beady eyes could be seen, and gave Parrot a very hard stare.

The next morning when he awoke there was a terrible pain in his mouth. It felt like someone was twisting and tugging on his teeth. "Oww, my teeth hurt!" he cried.

"Sssurely not!" hissed Snake, dangling down from a tree. "After all, you have sssuch perfect teeth!" and he slunk away again, snickering.

Snappy knew what he had to do. He set off down the river to visit Mr Drill the dentist.

It seemed such a long hard walk, and by the time he got there he was puffing and panting.

"Open wide!" said Mr Drill, an anteater, peering down his long nose into Snappy's gaping mouth. "Oh, dear. This doesn't look good at all. What have you been eating, Snappy? Now show me where it hurts."

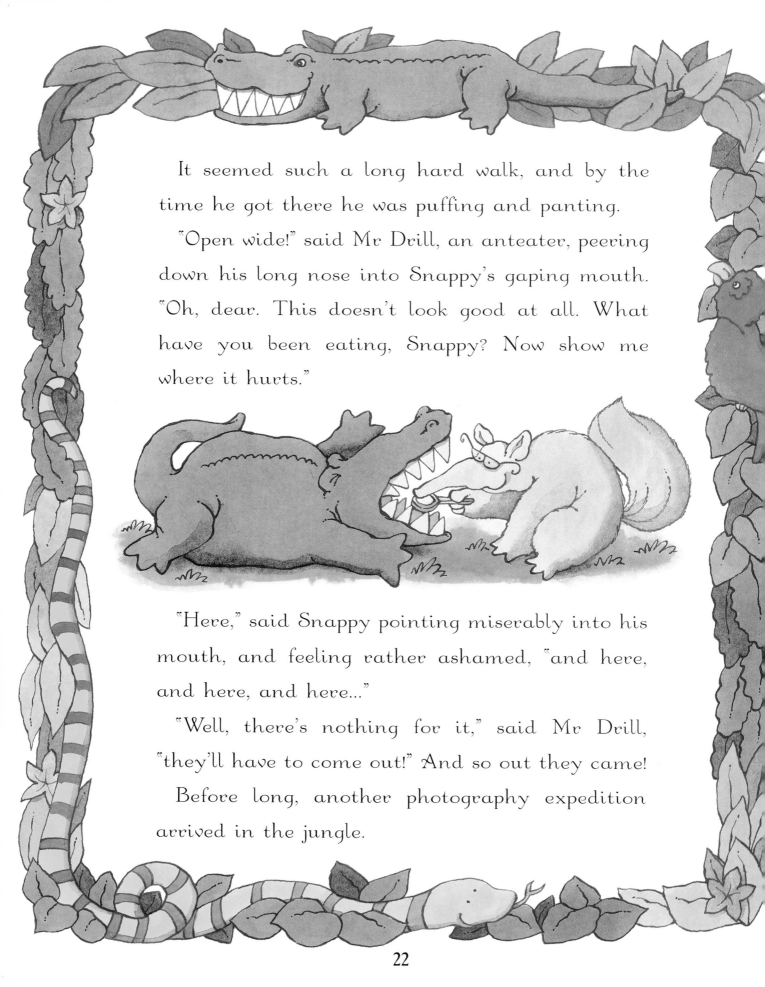

"Here," said Snappy pointing miserably into his mouth, and feeling rather ashamed, "and here, and here, and here..."

"Well, there's nothing for it," said Mr Drill, "they'll have to come out!" And so out they came!

Before long, another photography expedition arrived in the jungle.

"Say cheese!" said the expedition leader.

"CHEESE!" smiled Snappy, stepping out from behind a tree. But instead of a flash of cameras, Snappy met with howls of laughter, as the photographers fell about holding their sides.

"I thought you said Snappy was a handsome crocodile with perfect teeth!" they cried, looking at the leader. "He should be called Gappy, not Snappy!"

Poor Snappy slunk away into the bushes and cried. It was all his own fault for being so greedy and eating all that chocolate.

"There, there," said Mr Drill, patting his arm. "We'll soon fit you out with some fine new teeth."

And from then on, Snappy vowed he would never eat chocolate again!

NIPPY SNIPPY

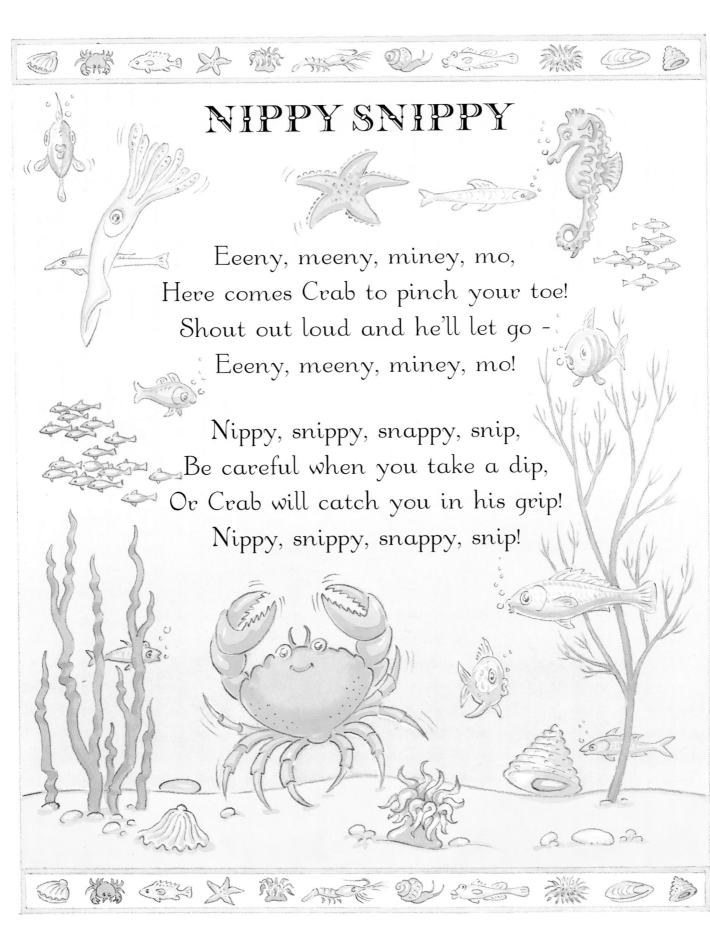

Eeeny, meeny, miney, mo,
Here comes Crab to pinch your toe!
Shout out loud and he'll let go -
Eeeny, meeny, miney, mo!

Nippy, snippy, snappy, snip,
Be careful when you take a dip,
Or Crab will catch you in his grip!
Nippy, snippy, snappy, snip!

ACHOO!

Mouse's eyes filled up with water,
His little nose started to twitch,
A tingling tickled his whiskers,
And then his knees started to itch.

He got a bad case of the hiccups,
Then threw back his head in a sneeze,
And he said, "I'm most awfully sorry,
It's just I'm allergic to cheese!"

THE COW WHO JUMPED OVER THE MOON

Boing, boing, boing! Bouncy Bunny kicked up her heels and bounded across the field.

"I can bounce high in the air, watch me!" she called to the other animals on the farm. Her fluffy white tail bobbed up and down.

"Very good!" said Silly Sheep, who was easily impressed.

"Yes, very good," said Swift, the sheepdog. "But not as good as me. I can jump right over the gate."

With that, he leapt over the gate and into the field.

"Amazing!" said Silly Sheep.

"Yes, amazing," said Harry Horse, with a flick of his mane. "But not as amazing as me. I can jump right over that hedge. Watch me!" And with that, he galloped around the field, then leapt high into the air, and sailed over the tall hedge.

"Unbelievable!" said Silly Sheep.

"Yes, unbelievable," said Daisy, the cow, chewing lazily on a clump of grass. "But not as unbelievable as me. I can jump right over the moon!"

"Well, I'm afraid that is unbelievable, Daisy," said Harry Horse. "No one can jump over the moon. That's just a fairy story."

"Well, I can," said Daisy, stubbornly. "And I can prove it! You can watch me do it if you like!"

The other animals all agreed that they would very much like to see Daisy jump over the moon.

"Meet me here in the field tonight, then," said Daisy to them. "When the moon is full, and the stars are shining bright."

So that night, when the moon had risen high up in the sky, the excited animals gathered together in the field. The rest of the animals from the farm came along too, for word had soon spread that Daisy the cow was going to jump over the moon, and they were all eager to watch.

"Come along then, Daisy," said Swift, the sheepdog, as the animals waited impatiently. "Are you going to show us how you can jump over the moon, or not?"

All the animals laughed, as they thought that Daisy was just boasting, and that she would not really be able to do it.

"Yes, I am going to show you," said Daisy, "but first of all, you will have to come with me. This isn't the right spot." Daisy led the animals across the field, to the far side, where a little stream ran along the edge of the field, separating it from the dark woods on the other side.

"Now, stand back everyone, and give me some room," said Daisy. The animals did as they were asked, and watched Daisy with anticipation, giggling nervously. Whatever was she going to do?

Daisy trotted back to the middle of the field, then ran towards the stream at a great speed.

At the last moment, she sprang into the air, and sailed across the stream, landing safely on the other side.

"I did it!" cried Daisy. "Aren't you going to clap, then?" The other animals looked at each other in confusion.

"But you only jumped over the stream!" said Harry Horse, puzzled.

"Come and take a closer look," called Daisy, still on the far side. The animals gathered close to the water's edge. They looked down, and there reflected in the water shimmered the great full moon! How the animals laughed when they realised Daisy had tricked them.

"See?" said Daisy. "I really can jump over the moon!" And just to prove it, she jumped back to the field again. The animals all clapped and cheered.

"That was a very good trick!" said Swift.

"Amazing!" said Silly Sheep. "Could someone explain it to me again, please!..."

HAPPY HIPPOPOTAMUS

Hey! look at me,
A happy hippopotamus,
Covered with mud
From my head to my bottom-us!
Squishing and squelching
And making an awful fuss,
Rolling around in my bath!

I like to blow bubbles
Breath out through my nose-es,
To wriggle and jiggle
The mud through my toes-es,
And would you believe it
That I smell like roses,
When I come out of my bath!

To the tune of 'Oh, dear, what can the matter be?'

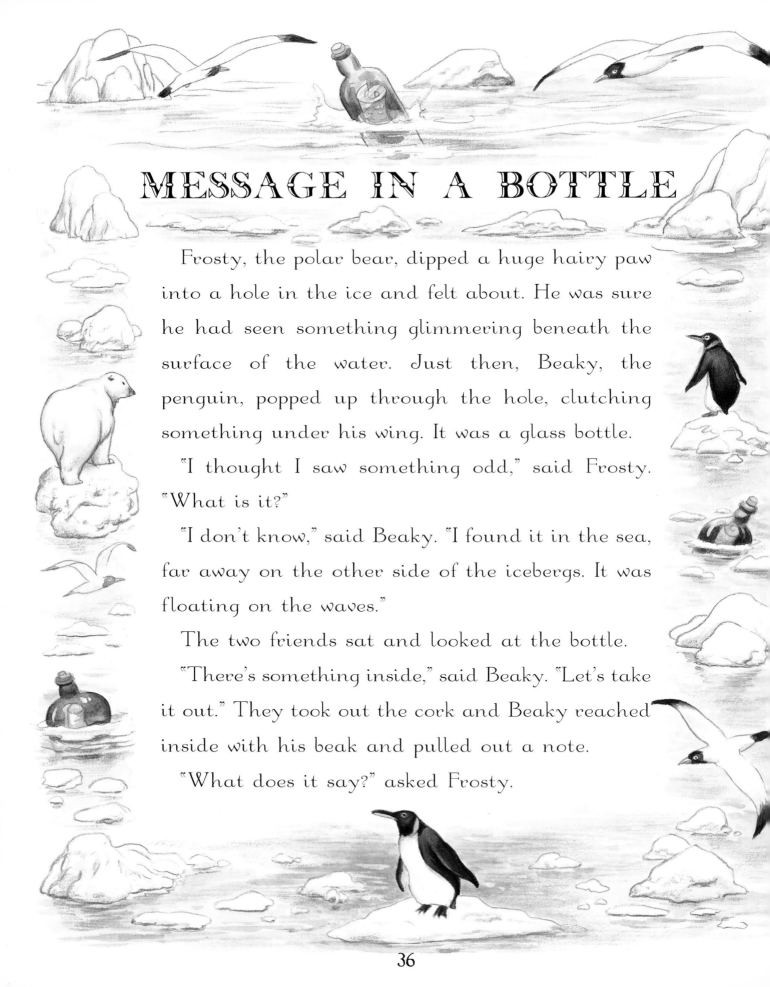

MESSAGE IN A BOTTLE

Frosty, the polar bear, dipped a huge hairy paw into a hole in the ice and felt about. He was sure he had seen something glimmering beneath the surface of the water. Just then, Beaky, the penguin, popped up through the hole, clutching something under his wing. It was a glass bottle.

"I thought I saw something odd," said Frosty. "What is it?"

"I don't know," said Beaky. "I found it in the sea, far away on the other side of the icebergs. It was floating on the waves."

The two friends sat and looked at the bottle.

"There's something inside," said Beaky. "Let's take it out." They took out the cork and Beaky reached inside with his beak and pulled out a note.

"What does it say?" asked Frosty.

Beaky peered closely at the note.

"It says: 'Help. I am stranded on a desert island. My boat is broken. It is very hot. Love Browny, the bear,'" read Beaky. "There's a map on the other side. Do you think we should help?"

"Of course we should," said Frosty. "It sounds like one of my cousins is in trouble. Anyway, it will be a great adventure! I've always wanted to know what hot feels like!"

The two friends studied the map carefully, then set off across the ice and snow until they reached the sea. They turned and waved goodbye to their chilly home, dived into the icy water and started to swim south in the direction of the desert island. After a while, Frosty began to feel tired. He had never swum so far away from home before.

"Let's rest a moment," said Beaky, and they flipped over in the water and lay floating along on their backs.

"Do you think it's much further?" asked Frosty.

"Oh, yes, much further," said Beaky. "The water has not even begun to get warm yet. By the time we get there it will be like taking a hot bath."

"I've never had one of those!" said Frosty, excitedly. "Will I like it?"

"I'm not sure," said Beaky.

So the two friends carried on swimming towards the sunshine. Gradually the water grew warmer and warmer. Frosty started to laugh.

"My skin's all nice and tingly," he chuckled.

On and on they swam. The bright sun beat down on their heads. By now Frosty was puffing and panting with every stroke.

"I think I must be feeling hot," he said. "I don't think I can swim much further!

"You don't have to!" said Beaky, pointing with his wing. "There's the island!"

On the shore, Browny was jumping up and down with excitement and waving his paws.

"You found me!" he cried. "Imagine my little bottle floating all the way to the North Pole!"

"Imagine me swimming all the way here from the North Pole!" panted Frosty, as he staggered out of the sea and collapsed in a heap on the hot sand. "I'm exhausted!"

Browny led his rescuers to the shelter of a cave he had found nearby, and they rested there until they recovered. As night fell, Browny built a fire on the beach, and they sat telling stories. He told them all about finding a little boat and setting sail across the sea, and how his boat had been shipwrecked.

"I thought I would be stranded here for ever!" Browny said. "And I want to go home!"

"Don't worry," said Frosty. "We'll get you home. But first let's get a good night's rest."

The next morning the three friends had great fun playing on the beach.

"I'm not sure I like hot, though," said Frosty, "it makes me tired and uncomfortable. And this sand stuff gets everywhere!" The others laughed.

"Let's be on our way then," said Beaky.

And so they set back off across the ocean, pulling Browny along on a raft he'd made, as he wasn't a good swimmer like the others. It was another long, hard journey, but when they finally reached Browny's home and saw how happy he was to be back there, they knew it was worth it.

"Promise you'll come and visit me again!" cried Browny, as the others waved goodbye and set off once more for their chilly home.

"We will!" cried Frosty. "But not if you're somewhere hot. I can't wait to get home for a good slide on the ice!"

FIVE LITTLE DUCKLINGS

One, two, three, four, five,
Five little ducklings duck and dive,
Six, seven, eight, nine, ten,
Then swim home in a row again!

Why do they swim in rows?
The answer is nobody knows!
I wonder, as they swim past,
Who goes first and who goes last?

To the tune of 'Once I Caught A Fish Alive.'

CAT'S CHORUS

We meet every night
On the same garden wall,
And if you're in luck
You may hear our call:
With howl and a yowl, and a hullaballoo,
We're the cat's chorus, singing for you!

Fifi's soprano,
Butch sings the bass,
Kipper's a baritone,
Bert sets the pace.

Chorus

We sing lots of songs
Both new ones and old,
All huddled together
To keep out the cold.

Chorus

BIRTHDAY BUNNIES

"It's my first birthday tomorrow!" announced Snowy, a little white rabbit, very proudly. "Isn't that exciting?"

"Yes, very exciting!" said Whiskers, her brother. "Because it's my birthday too!"

"And mine!" said Patch.

"And mine!" said Nibble.

"And mine!" said Twitch.

"Do you think mummy and daddy have got a surprise for us?" asked Snowy.

"I hope so!" said Whiskers.

"Me too!" said Patch.

"Me too!" said Nibble.

"Me too!" said Twitch.

Mrs Rabbit was listening outside the door, as her children were getting ready for bed. She heard the little bunnies chattering excitedly about their birthdays the next day.

Whatever could she do to make it a special day for them? She sat and thought very hard, and later that evening, when Mr Rabbit came home, she said: "It is the childrens' first birthday tomorrow, and I'm planning a surprise for them. I want to make them a carrot cake, but I will need some carrots. Could you go and dig some nice fresh ones up from your vegetable garden?"

"Certainly, dear," said Mr Rabbit, and off he went back outside.

Mr Rabbit was proud of the carrots he grew. They were very fine carrots, crunchy and sweet and delicious. Every year he entered them in the Country Show, and they nearly always won first prize. So you can imagine his dismay when he arrived at his vegetable patch to find that every single carrot had been dug up and stolen!

He marched back inside. "Someone has stolen my carrots!" he announced to his wife, crossly. "And I am going to find out just who it is!"

And although it was getting late, he went back outside, and set off to find the naughty person.

First of all he stopped at Hungry Hare's house, and knocked at the door.

"Someone has stolen my carrots!" Mr Rabbit said. "Do you know who?"

"Oh, yes," said Hungry Hare. "But it wasn't me." And although Mr Rabbit pressed him, Hungry Hare would say no more.

Next Mr Rabbit went to Sly Fox's house.

"Someone has stolen my carrots!" he said. "Do you know who?"

"Oh, yes," said Sly Fox. "But it wasn't me." And although Mr Rabbit begged and pleaded with him, Sly Fox would say no more.

So Mr Rabbit marched to Bill Badger's house, and asked if he knew who had taken the carrots.

"Why, yes, in fact I do," said Bill Badger. "But it wasn't me."

And just like the others, he would say no more. It was the same wherever Mr Rabbit went, and although he got very cross, and stamped his foot, no one would tell him who had stolen his carrots!

"You'll find out soon enough," said Red Squirrel.

So Mr Rabbit went home feeling very puzzled.

"It seems that everyone knows who it was, but no one will tell me!" said Mr Rabbit to his wife.

"Not everyone, dear," she said. "I don't know who it was either. All I know is that it's our childrens' first birthday tomorrow, and we have no surprise for them." And feeling very miserable and confused, they went to bed, determined to get to the bottom of the mystery in the morning.

Next day the little bunnies came running into the kitchen, where their parents were having breakfast.

"Happy birthday, everyone!" called Snowy.

"Happy birthday!" cried the other little bunnies.

"Now, it's not much, but I wanted to give each of you a surprise!" Snowy went on. "By the way, I hope you don't mind, Dad." And with that Snowy pulled out a box of juicy carrots, each tied with a bow, and handed one to each of her brothers and sisters.

"Snap!" cried Whiskers, "I had just the same idea!" and he pulled out another box of carrots.

"Me too!" said Patch.

"Me too!" said Nibble.

"Me too!" said Twitch.

Soon there was a great pile of juicy carrots heaped on the kitchen table.

"So that's what happened to my carrots!" cried Mr Rabbit, in amazement. "I thought they had been stolen! And when he told the little bunnies the story they laughed till their sides ached. Then Mrs Rabbit put on her apron and shooed them outside.

"Just leave the carrots with me," she said.
"I have a birthday surprise of my own in store!"

And so the mystery was solved. It turned out that Hungry Hare had seen the little bunnies creep out one by one, and each dig up a few carrots when they thought no one was looking. He knew it was their birthdays and he guessed what they were doing. He had told the other forest folk, and everyone thought it was a great joke.

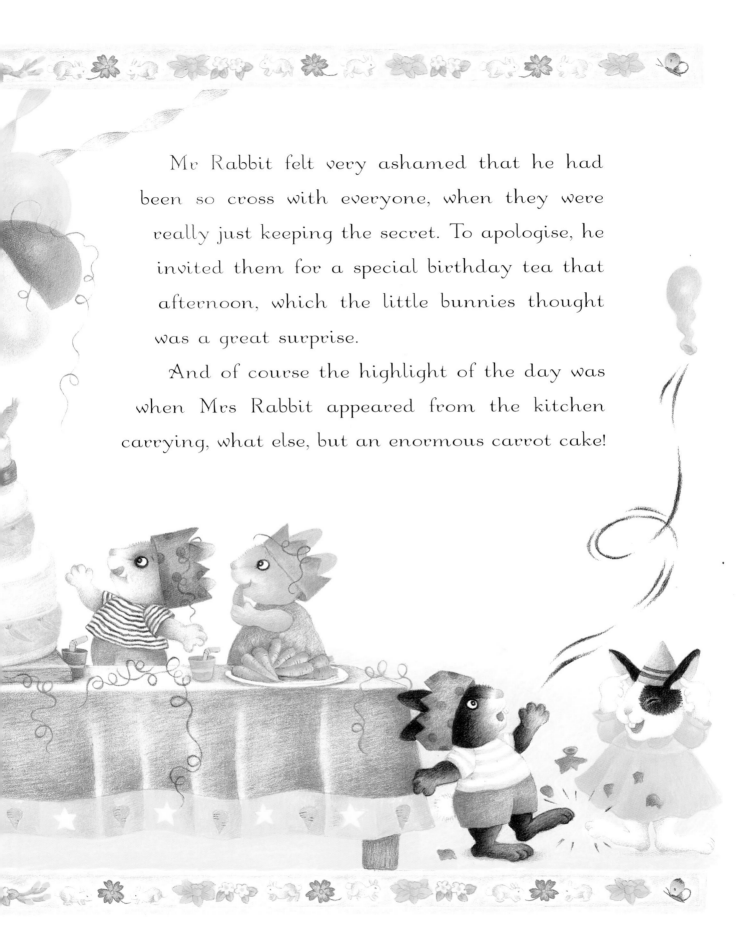

Mr Rabbit felt very ashamed that he had been so cross with everyone, when they were really just keeping the secret. To apologise, he invited them for a special birthday tea that afternoon, which the little bunnies thought was a great surprise.

And of course the highlight of the day was when Mrs Rabbit appeared from the kitchen carrying, what else, but an enormous carrot cake!

HIGH JUMP

The Shrew said to the Kangaroo,
"I can jump as high as you!"
Laughed Kanga, "How can that be true
Of one so small, please tell me, do!"

Said Shrew, "I'll show you, then you'll see,
I'll jump so high, I'll reach that tree!
But first of all you must agree,
To show your jumping skills to me!"

Then Kanga bounced into the air,
So busy he was unaware
That Shrew was clinging to his hair
To reach the treetop – most unfair!

Back Kanga landed on the ground,
"Your turn," he said, and spun around.
"Up here!" called Shrew, a distant sound.
"Well," said Kanga, "I'll be bound!"

LAZY LION

Lazy Lion lay snoozing in the shade of a tree. The hot sun beat down, as he lazily flicked at the buzzing flies with his tail.

There was nothing Lazy Lion liked to do more than sleep. He would sleep all night and all day if he could, just waking up every once in a while to have a snack.

"Hmm," he purred to himself. "This is the life. Nothing to do all day but lie in the sun and sleep. Perfect!"

Just then, a laughing hyena came running by.

"Wake up, Lazy Lion!" he chuckled. "Unless you feel like going for a swim!? Rain's coming!"

Lazy Lion opened one eye. "Silly creature!" he said with a sniff, as he watched the hyena running far off into the distance, still laughing. "He's just trying to trick me into waking up and moving!" and he closed his eyes and went back to sleep.

A short while later someone nudged his behind.

"Wake up, Lazy Lion. Rain's coming." Giraffe was bending her long neck down and nudging him with her nose. "You should head for shelter. The river might flood!"

"Don't be ridiculous!" said Lion. "Hyena's been filling your head with his nonsense, I see!" and he closed his eyes and was snoring again in seconds.

But he had not been dozing for long when he felt something tugging at his whiskers.

"Wake up, Lazy Lion!" It was a little mouse.

"Rain's coming. Could you please carry my children and I to safety?" asked the mouse.

"Oh, I'm far too busy for that," said Lazy Lion. "Besides, what's all this talk of rain? It's a fine, sunny day!" And with that, he closed his eyes and went back to sleep.

A few moments later he was woken by something pulling at his tail. It was Monkey.

"Wake up, Lazy Lion. Rain's coming. Could you help carry my bananas up to the rocks?"

"Why does everyone keep waking me?" asked Lazy Lion, crossly. "Can't you see I'm busy?"

"Sorry, Lion, but you didn't look busy to me," said Monkey.

"Well, I am!" growled Lion. "I'm very busy thinking what to do with the next person who wakes me up!" And he gave Monkey a mean stare, before shutting his eyes tight once more.

After that, none of the animals dared to wake Lazy Lion up again. So they couldn't warn him that the dark storm clouds were gathering, and the first drops of rain had started to fall.

They just hurried high up to the safety of the rocks and caves and took shelter from the storm that was on its way.

Lazy Lion gave a little shiver, as he lay dreaming. A big raindrop fell on his nose. Then another, and another. Lion stirred. "Oh, bother," he thought to himself. "It's raining. Well, it's probably only a light shower. I'll snooze a little longer." He settled back down to sleep.

But the rain began to fall harder, and harder. Soon Lazy Lion's thick fur was wet through, and he was starting to feel cold and uncomfortable. But he was still too lazy to get up and move to the shelter of the rocks. "I'll just sleep for five more minutes!" he told himself.

But as the minutes passed the rain fell harder and harder, and the river rose higher and higher. Then, with a huge crash of thunder, and a bright flash of lightening, the river broke its banks and came flooding across the plains! All of a sudden, Lazy Lion found himself being tossed around as he struggled to keep his head above the stormy waters.

The other animals watched in horror from the safety of the rocks as Lazy Lion was dragged below the water by the strong current.

Then suddenly his big strong head popped up again, and he gasped for breath.

Lazy Lion swam with all his might towards the rocks, as the other animals cheered him on.

"Oh, this is hard work!" he panted. How he wished he had listened to the others and had not been so lazy.

At last he made it, and he struggled up onto the rocks, wet through and worn out. The other animals gathered round, anxiously.

"Are you all right, Lazy Lion?" asked Monkey.

"I'm exhausted!" panted Lazy Lion, then added, "But it's nothing a good sleep won't cure!"

ELEPHANTS NEVER FORGET

I woke up this morning, astounded,
To find my long trunk in a knot!
I know it must be to remind me
To remember something I've forgot!

But though I've been thinking all morning
I haven't remembered it yet.
Still I'm sure I will think of it soon,
Because elephants never forget!

ITCHY SPOTS

Poor Monkey was wriggling
And jiggling around,
Scratching and making
A chattering sound:

"They're driving me mad,
Someone help me please –
I have to get rid of
These terrible fleas!"

Then along came a bear
In a bit of a stew –
"I've got such a bad itch,
I don't know what to do!

It's right in a spot
I can't reach with my paws.
So why not scratch my back,
And I will scratch yours!"

WHALE SONG

"Oh, what a beautiful morning!" sang Flippy, the whale, as streaks of sunlight filtered down through the clear blue ocean. He swam to and fro, twirled around, then whooshed up through the waves, and jumped clear of the water in a perfect pirouette.

Flippy loved to sing and dance. The trouble was, although he was a very graceful dancer, his singing was terrible. His big mouth would open wide, as he boomed out song after song — but none of them were in tune! The dreadful sound echoed through the ocean for miles, sending all the fish and other ocean creatures diving into the rocks and reefs for cover, as the waters shook around them. It was always worse when the sun shone, as the bright warm sun made Flippy want to sing and dance with happiness. It had got so bad that the other creatures had begun to pray for dull skies and rain.

"Something has got to be done!" complained Wobble, the jellyfish. "Flippy's booming voice makes me quiver and shake so much that I can't see where I'm going!"

"Well, I know where I'm going," said Snappy, the lobster. "As far away as possible. My head is splitting from Flippy's awful wailing."

"Someone will have to tell Flippy not to sing anymore," said Sparky, the stingray.

"But it will hurt his feelings," said Wobble.

"Not as much as his singing hurts my ears!" snapped Snappy.

And so they decided that Sparky would tell Flippy the next day that they did not want him to sing any more songs. Wobble was right. Flippy was very upset when he heard that the others did not like his singing. He cried big, salty tears.

"I was only trying to enjoy myself!" he sobbed. "I didn't realise I was upsetting everyone else."

"There, there," said Sparky, wishing he had not been chosen to give the little whale the bad news. "You can still enjoy dancing."

"It's not the same without music," said Flippy, miserably. "You can't get the rhythm." And he swam off into the deep waters, saying he wanted to be alone for a while.

As Flippy lay on the bottom of the ocean floor, feeling very sorry for himself, a beautiful sound came floating through the water from far away in the distance. It sounded like someone singing. Flippy wanted to know who was making such a lovely sound, so with a flick of his big tail, he set off in the direction it was coming from.

As he got closer, he could hear a soft voice singing a beautiful melody. Peering out from behind a big rock, he saw that the voice belonged to a little octopus, who was shuffling and swaying about on the ocean floor. His legs seemed to be going in all directions, as he stumbled and tripped along.

Then he tried to spin around, but his legs got tangled and he crashed to the ground in a heap.

"Oh, dear," said Leggy, the octopus. "I seem to have eight left feet!"

Flippy looked out shyly from behind the rock.

"What are you trying to do?" he asked.

The little octopus looked rather embarrassed.

"I was trying to dance," he said, blushing pink. "Only I'm not very good at it."

"Well, maybe I could teach you," said Flippy. "I'm a very good dancer. And in return, there is something that I would love you to teach me!.."

A few weeks later, Wobble, Snappy and Sparky were discussing how they missed having Flippy around, when they heard a strange and beautiful sound floating towards them through the ocean.

"Oh, what a beautiful morning..." came the song, only this time there were two voices singing in perfect harmony!

"Surely that can't be Flippy!" said the others in surprise. But to their amazement, as the voices came closer they saw that, sure enough, it was Flippy, spinning and twirling as he danced gracefully towards them with his new friend!

LITTLE SHEEP

Little Sheep couldn't sleep,
Not a wink, not a peep!
Tossing, turning, all night through,
What was poor Little Sheep to do?

Owl came by, old and wise,
Said, "Silly sheep, use your eyes –
You're lying in a field of sheep,
Try counting them to help you sleep!"

"Seven, four, thirteen, ten –
That's not right, I'll start again..."
Till daylight came, awake he lay
And vowed he'd learn to count next day!

GIRAFFE'S SONG

It's wonderful having a long neck,
That reaches right up to the sky,
You can nibble the leaves on the treetops,
And smile at the birds flying by.

It's wonderful having a long neck,
You can see for miles around,
You always know just where
your friends are,
And where the best food can be found.

It's wonderful having a long neck,
Although, I'm not meaning to gloat.
For there's one time that I really curse it,
And that's when I get a sore throat!

LEAP FROG

"Whee! Look at me! Look at me!" yelled Springy, the frog, as he went leaping through the air, jumping from one lily pad to the other with a great splash. "I'm the bounciest frog in the whole wide world! Whee!"

"Tut, tut!" quacked Mother Duck. "That young frog is a nuisance. He never looks where he's going, and he doesn't mind who he splashes."

"Quite dreadful," agreed Downy, the swan. "And he makes so much noise. Sometimes it's hard to hear yourself think!"

But Springy wasn't listening. He was far too busy jumping across the lily pads as high as he could.

"Come on!" he called to the little ducklings. "Come over here, we'll have a diving contest!"

The ducklings shook their tails with excitement as they hurried across the pond towards him, then splashed about ducking and diving.

"He's a bad influence on our youngsters," Mother Duck went on. "If only something could be done about him."

"I suppose it's just high spirits," said Downy. "He'll grow out of it."

But Springy didn't grow out of it — he grew worse. He would wake everyone up at the crack of dawn, singing loudly at the top of his croaky voice:

"Here comes the day, it's time to play, hip hooray, hip hooray!" And he would leap from place to place, waking up the ducks and swans in their nests, calling down Rabbit's burrow, and shouting into Water Rat's hole in the bank. Of course, Springy just thought that he was being friendly. He didn't realise that everyone was getting fed up with him.

"I'm all for a bit of fun," said Water Rat. "But young Springy always takes things too far."

Then one day, Springy appeared almost bursting with excitement.

"Listen everyone," he called. "There's going to be a jumping competition on the other side of the pond. All the other frogs from miles around are coming. But I'm sure to win, because I'm the bounciest frog in the whole wide world!" And with that he jumped high up in the air, just to prove it was true.

The day of the contest dawned, and everyone gathered at the far side of the pond to watch the competition. Springy had never seen so many frogs in one place before.

"Wait till they see how high I can jump!" he said, leaping up and down in excitement.

But to Springy's amazement, all the frogs could jump high, and far too. They sprang gracefully across the lily pads, cheered on by the crowd.

Springy was going to have to jump higher and further than ever if he wanted to win. At last it was his turn. "Good luck!" cried the ducklings.

Springy took his place on the starting pad, then gathering all his strength, he leapt up high and flew through the air, further and further, past the finish line, and on, until — GULP! He landed right in crafty Pike's waiting open mouth! As usual, Springy had not been looking where he was going!

The naughty pike swallowed Springy in one gulp, then dived down and hid in the middle of the pond. Everyone looked around in dismay — there was nothing they could do. Springy was gone.

Well, there was no doubt about it. Springy had jumped the highest, and the furthest.

"I declare Springy the winner," Warty, the toad, who had organised the contest, said glumly. So everyone went home, feeling sad and empty.

After that, things were much quieter for the other folk that lived around the pond.

But instead of enjoying the peace, they found that they rather missed Springy.

"He was a cheery little frog," said Downy.

"My young ones miss him terribly," said Mother Duck. "I suppose he did keep them busy."

But deep in the pond, Pike was feeling sorry for himself. He thought he'd been very clever catching that frog, but he'd had terrible indigestion ever since. You see, Springy was still busy jumping away inside him! Pike rose up to the top of the water, and gulped at the air. And as he did so, out jumped Springy!

Everyone was delighted to see him, and cheered as they gave him the medal for winning the jumping contest.

"This is wonderful," said Springy. "But I have learned my lesson — from now on I'll look before I leap!" and he hopped away quietly to play with the ducklings.

LITTLE DOG LOST

"Brrr," shivered Scruffy. "It's cold tonight."

"Well, snuggle up closer to me," said his mum.

"It's not fair," Scruffy grumbled. "Why do we have to sleep outside in the cold? The cats are allowed to sleep inside, in nice warm baskets!"

"We're farm dogs, dear," said Mum. "We have to be tough, and work hard to earn our keep."

"I'd rather be a cat," mumbled Scruffy. "All they do is wash themselves, eat and sleep."

"We don't have such a bad life," said Mum. "Now stop feeling sorry for yourself, and get some rest. We've got a lot of work to do tomorrow."

The next day, Scruffy woke early and trotted down the lane for a walk. He ran through the grass, chasing rabbits, and sniffing at the flowers.

Now, usually when he got to the end of the lane he stopped and turned back. But today, he saw a big red van parked outside a house there. The back of the van was open, and Scruffy thought he would just climb inside and take a look.

The van was full of furniture. At the back was a big armchair with soft cushions. Scruffy clambered onto it. "I could doze all day, like a cat!" he told himself. He closed his eyes and before he knew it he had fallen fast asleep.

Scruffy awoke some time later with a sharp jolt.
"Oh, no, I fell asleep!" he groaned. "I'd better hurry back. We've got a busy day ahead!"

But then he saw that the van doors were closed! He could hear voices outside.

"Oh, dear, I'll be in trouble if I get found in here," thought Scruffy, and he hid behind the chair.

The back of the van opened and Scruffy peered out. Two men started unloading the furniture.

When Scruffy was sure that no one was looking, he crept out of the van, but he was no longer in the countryside where he lived! He was in a big noisy town, full of buildings and cars.

Poor Scruffy had no idea where he was!

"The van must have carried me away," thought Scruffy, feeling frightened.

All day long, Scruffy roamed around trying to find his way home, feeling cold, tired and hungry. At last, he lay down and began to howl miserably.

"What's the matter, pup?" he heard a man's kind voice say. "You look lost. Come home with me." Scruffy gave the man's hand a grateful lick, then jumped up and followed him home.

When they arrived at the man's house Scruffy sat on the doorstep, hoping the man might bring him some food out to eat. But the man said, "Come on in, you can't stay out there."

Scruffy followed the man in, and found a little poodle waiting to meet him. Scruffy stared at her in amazement. What had happened to her fur?

"You'd better take a bath before supper," said the man, looking at Scruffy's dirty white coat. The man washed him in a big tub, then brushed his tangled coat. Scruffy howled miserably. What had he done to deserve such punishment?

"Don't you like it?" asked the poodle, shyly.

"No, I don't," said Scruffy. "All this washing and cleaning is for cats!"

Next the man gave them supper — small bowls of dry pellets. Scruffy sniffed at them in disgust. He was used to chunks of meat and a nice big bone.

"This looks like cat food," said Scruffy, miserably.

After supper the poodle climbed into a big basket in the kitchen.

"I thought that belonged to a cat," said Scruffy. He tried sleeping in the basket but he was hot and uncomfortable. He missed counting the stars to help him fall asleep, and most of all he missed his mum.

"I want to go home," he cried, and big tears slipped down his nose.

The next day, the man put Scruffy on a lead and took him into town. He hated being dragged along, without being able to sniff at things.

Then, as they crossed the market place, Scruffy heard a familiar bark, and saw his mum's head hanging through the window of the farmer's truck! He started to howl, dragged the man over to where the truck was parked, then leapt up at the window barking excitedly. The farmer could hardly believe it was Scruffy — he had never seen him so clean! The man explained how he had found Scruffy, and the farmer thanked the man for taking such good care of him.

On the way back home, Scruffy told his mum all about his adventure and what had happened.

"I thought you had run away because you didn't like being a farm dog," she said gently.

"Oh, no, Mum," said Scruffy, quickly. "I love being a farm dog. I can't wait to get home to a nice big juicy bone and our little bed beneath the stars!"

THE END

Illustrations by:
Stephanie Boey, Mario Capaldi,
Maggie Downer, Serena Feneziani,
Andrew Geeson, Piers Harper,
Elaine Keary, Claire Mumford,
Jessica Stockham.